This Little Tiger book belongs to:

Aidenn Jadav

For Joshua David Constant
and Hannah Linda Constant,
with love ~ *LC*

For Noah ~ *JC*

LITTLE TIGER PRESS
An imprint of Magi Publications
1 The Coda Centre, 189 Munster Road, London SW6 6AW, UK
www.littletigerpress.com
First published in Great Britain 2000
by Little Tiger Press, London
This edition published 2008
Text copyright © Linda Cornwell 2000
Illustrations copyright © Jane Chapman 2000
Linda Cornwell and Jane Chapman have asserted their rights
to be identified as the author and illustrator of this work
under the Copyright, Designs and Patents Act, 1988.
All rights reserved • ISBN 978-1-84506-895-0
Printed in China
3 5 7 9 10 8 6 4

Two Hungry Bears

Linda Cornwell and Jane Chapman

LITTLE TIGER PRESS

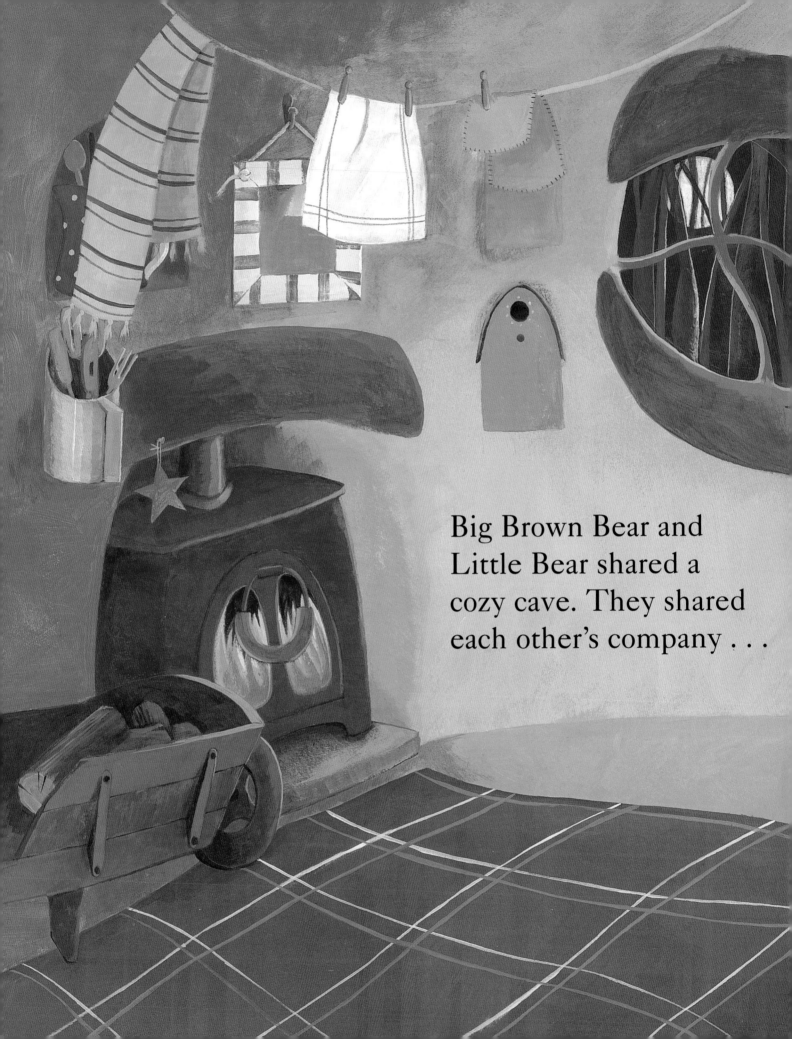

Big Brown Bear and
Little Bear shared a
cozy cave. They shared
each other's company . . .

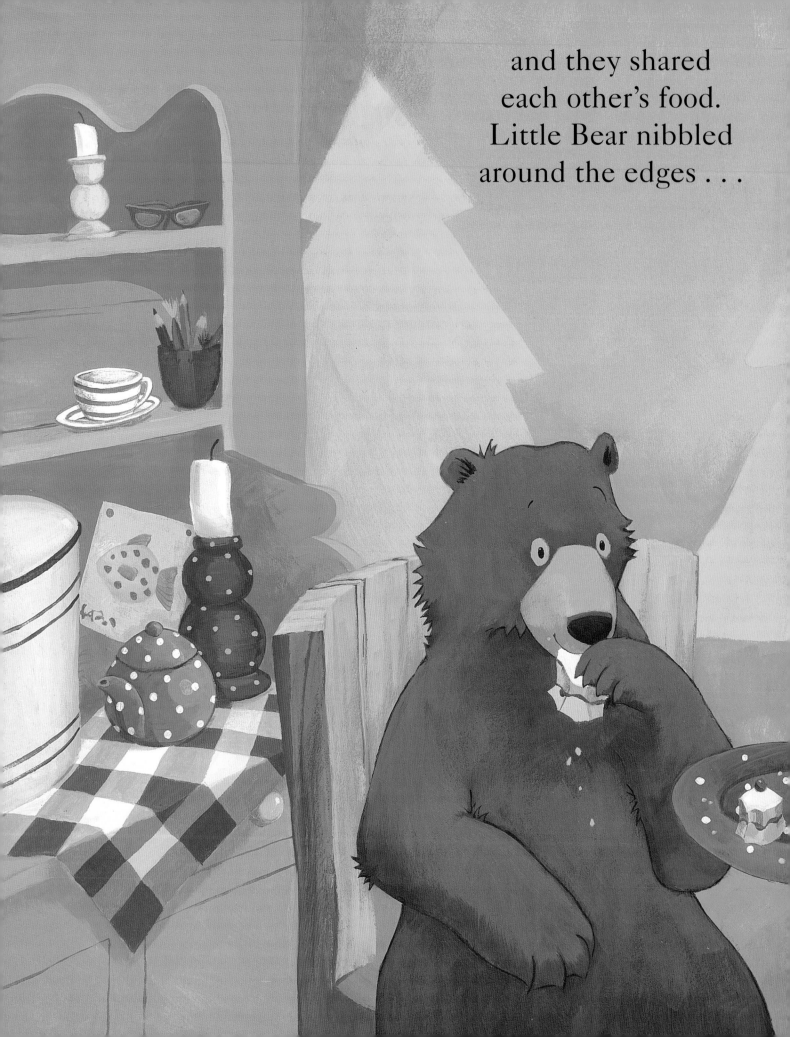

and they shared
each other's food.
Little Bear nibbled
around the edges . . .

and Big Brown Bear
munched up the middles.
In this way, they got
along very well.

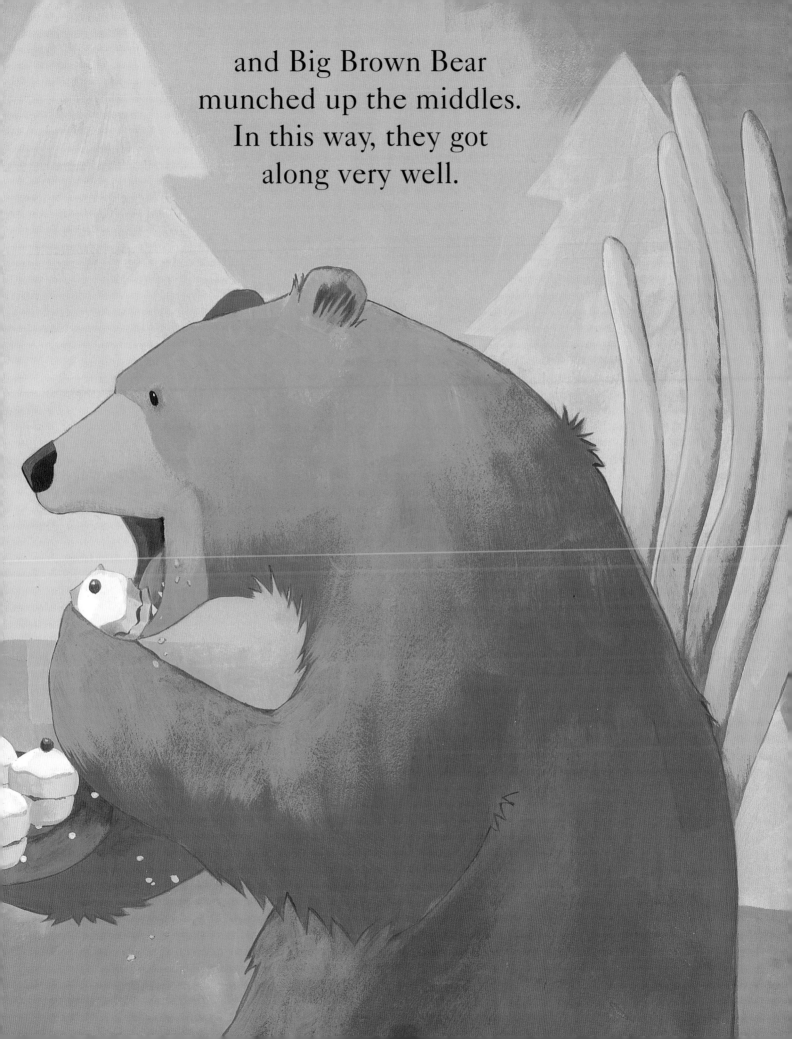

But one bright autumn day, Little Bear woke up feeling EXTRA hungry and Big Brown Bear woke up feeling MONSTROUSLY hungry!

"I'll buy some food for both of us," said Little Bear.

"That's very kind of you, Little Bear," answered Big Brown Bear sleepily, and he crept right back to bed.

Little Bear went out
shopping and bought
some things to take
back to Big Brown
Bear. But she found
she was so hungry . . .

that she ate everything
straight away—
pies and pastries,
peanuts and puddings,

chocolates and cheeses,
crisps and cakes—

from sides to middles,
middles to sides
AND BACK AGAIN!

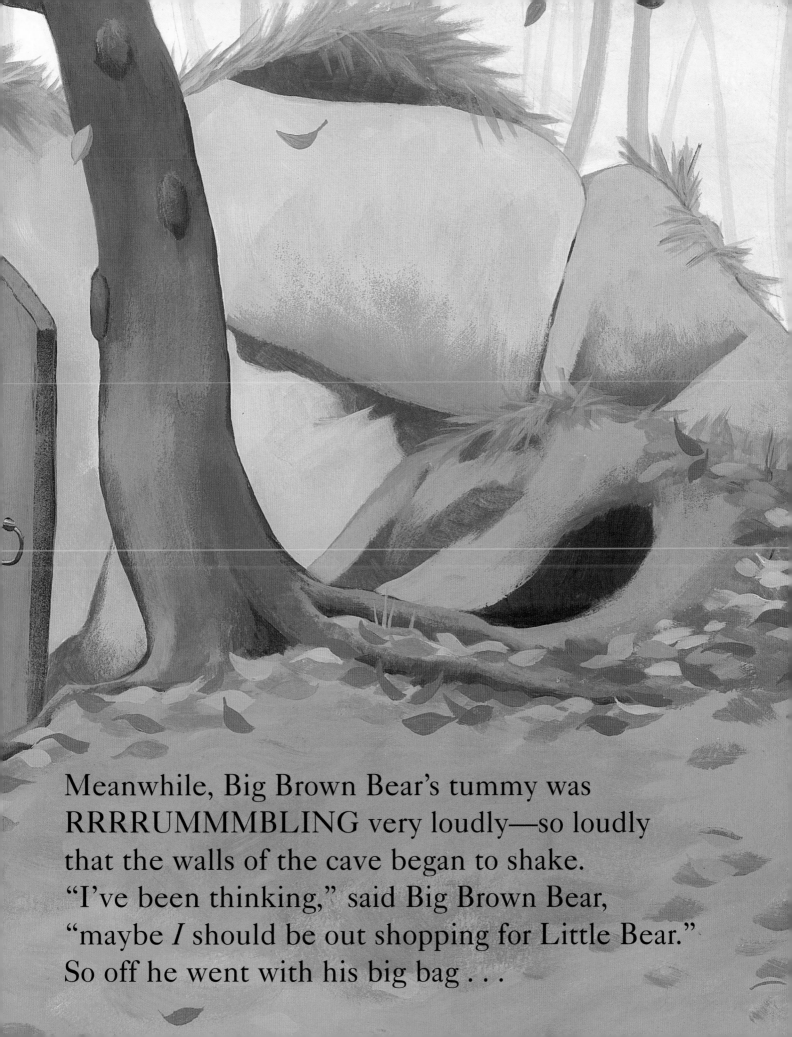

Meanwhile, Big Brown Bear's tummy was
RRRRUMMMBLING very loudly—so loudly
that the walls of the cave began to shake.
"I've been thinking," said Big Brown Bear,
"maybe *I* should be out shopping for Little Bear."
So off he went with his big bag . . .

but when he had filled
it right up, he found
he was so hungry,
he could not wait.

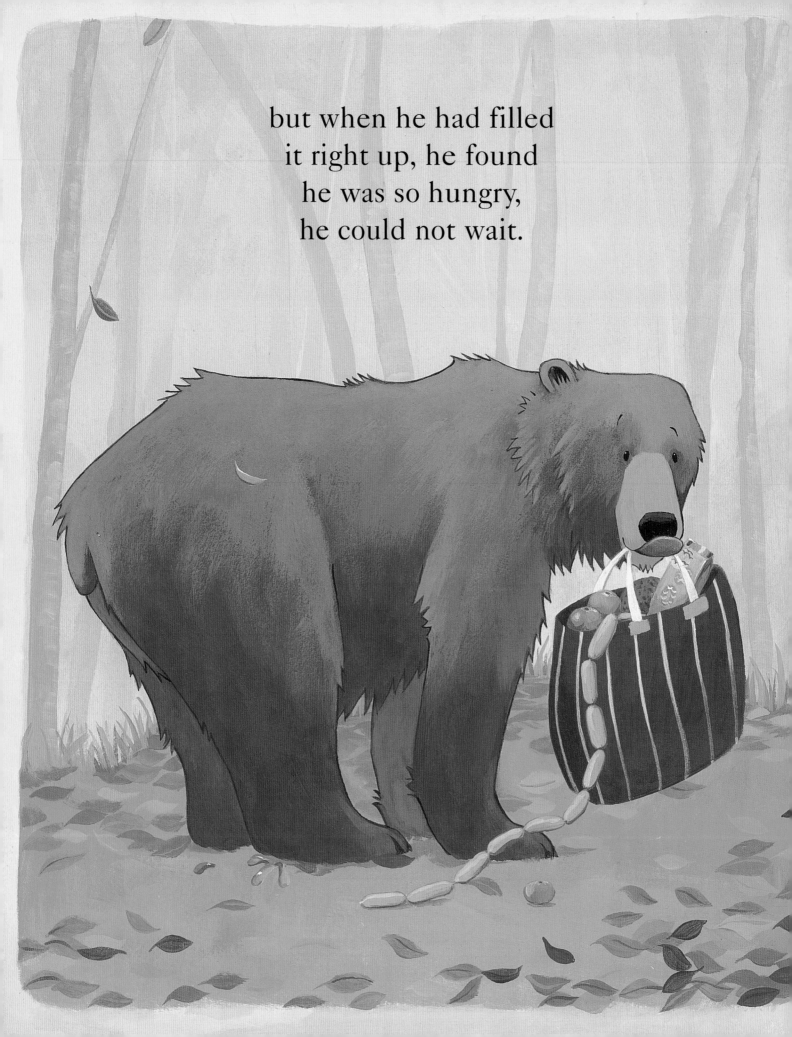

He began by
munching just
the middles.

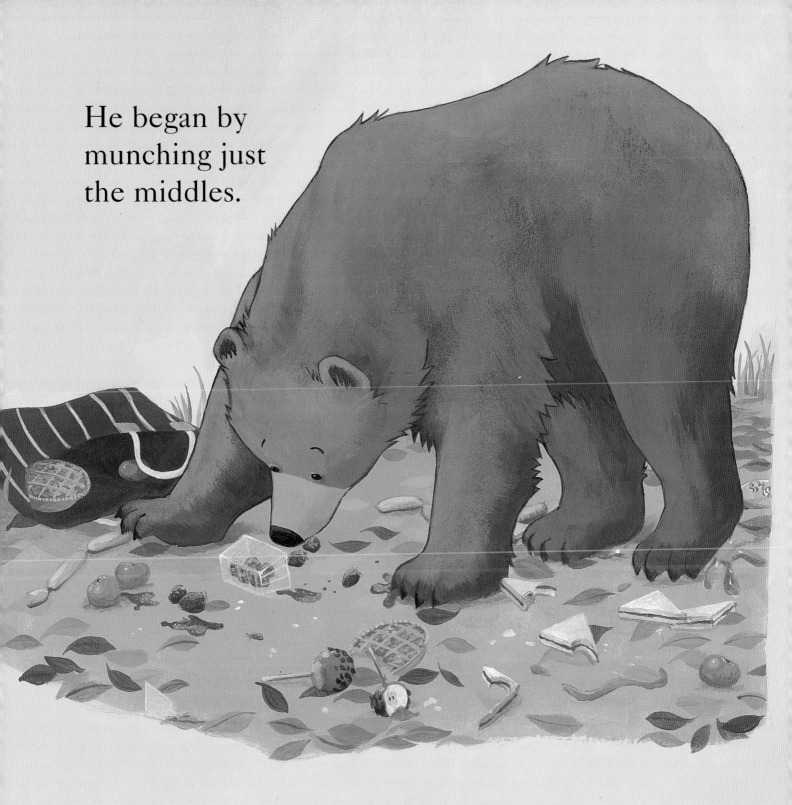

But then he set to work on sausages,
strawberries and sandwiches,
not to mention tangerines,
caramel apples and peach pies . . .

AND hamburgers, custard and fries . . .

AND biscuits, spaghetti and soup . . .

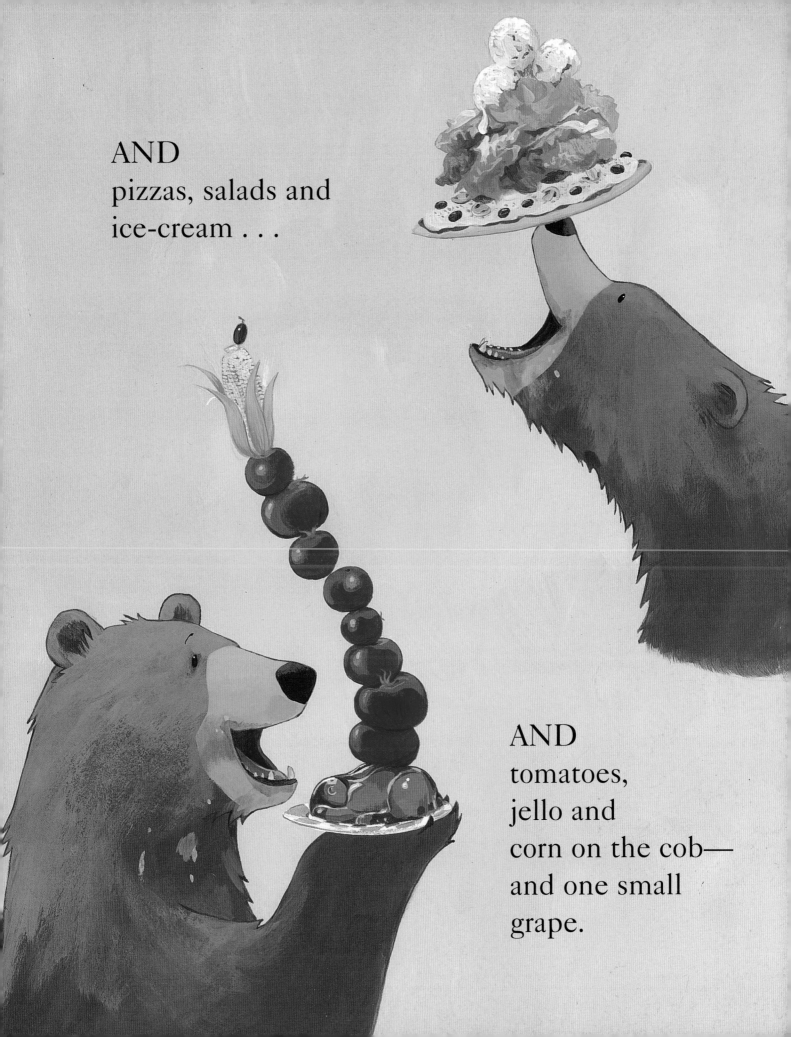

AND
pizzas, salads and
ice-cream . . .

AND
tomatoes,
jello and
corn on the cob—
and one small
grape.

Big Brown Bear ate tops, bottoms,
sides, and middles.
There was just no stopping him!

But when he had finished eating,
he began to feel very, very full
and very, very guilty.
He had nothing left for Little Bear.

Big Brown Bear staggered back home where
Little Bear was waiting patiently for him.
"Did you find any nice middles to munch?"
Little Bear asked him. *I can see that you did!*
she thought to herself.
Big Brown Bear could only nod his head.

"Did you come across any tasty edges to nibble?"
asked Big Brown Bear. *It certainly looks as
though you might have!* he thought to himself.

They sat
down together—
very carefully.
"I saved you half
of a cracker,"
said Big Brown Bear.
"It still has four
edges to nibble."
"I saved you three
quarters of a banana,"
said Little Bear.
"It's all middle—
no edges
at all!"

After a while, Big Brown Bear yawned. "I think I'll skip supper," he said. "I'm feeling a little too tired." "An early night will do us both good," agreed Little Bear. They spent an awfully long time brushing their teeth . . .

before Big Brown Bear snuggled into his
bed, and Little Bear crept quietly into hers.
"Let's buy the food together tomorrow,"
said Big Brown Bear with a yawn.
But tomorrow was a long, long time away
because . . .

Big Brown Bear and
Little Bear slept, with
their tummies pleasantly full,
all through the winter until
SPRING!

Fantastic reads from Little Tiger Press

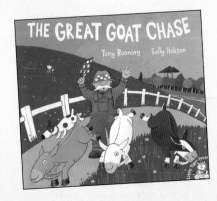

For information regarding any of the above titles
or for our catalogue, please contact us:
Little Tiger Press, 1 The Coda Centre,
189 Munster Road, London SW6 6AW, UK
Tel: +44 (0)20 7385 6333 Fax: +44 (0)20 7385 7333
E-mail: info@littletiger.co.uk
www.littletigerpress.com